I0434167

More Spaghetti!

Story by Annette Smith

Illustrations by Meredith Thomas

Tommy was happy today.

He was going to stay
at his friend Robert's house
for the night.

But Tommy was a little bit scared, too.

He had stayed at his gran's house,
but he had never stayed
with a friend before.

"Hello, Tommy," smiled Robert's mother.
"Come on in.
I'm pleased you have come to stay.
You can put your bag in Robert's room.
Then I will get you something to eat."

The boys went into Robert's bedroom.

Tommy looked around the room.

"Mum has made up
this bed for you," said Robert.
"It's a good bed," he laughed,
jumping on it. "Look!"

Tommy tried to laugh.
But he was feeling scared
and now he wanted to go home.

Robert's mother gave them
some milk and a banana each.

"Thank you," said Tommy.
"I like bananas."

"Good," said Robert's mother.
"I hope you like spaghetti, too,
because we are having it
for dinner."

Tommy loved spaghetti!
He began to feel much better.

The boys got out
Robert's racing cars and truck
to play with until dinner time.

Then Robert said,
"My mum makes the best spaghetti."

Tommy looked at Robert.
"But you don't make spaghetti!
You get it out of a can!" he said.

"Not our spaghetti," said Robert.
"You wait until you try **ours**!"

But Tommy didn't want to try it.
He liked spaghetti out of a can.

Then Robert's father came home
from work.
"I can smell something good cooking,"
he said with a smile.

At dinner time,
Tommy sat beside Robert's mother.
Tommy looked at his bowl.
He had never seen spaghetti
like this before.

Everyone began to eat.
Tommy ate a little. It was **very** good!

Tommy ate some more spaghetti.
"I love it," he smiled,
"but it keeps slipping off my fork!"

"It always slips off my fork, too,"
said Robert, and everyone laughed.

"Would you like some more?"
asked Robert's mother.

"Yes, please," said Tommy.
"I like it here at your place."